Do You See a Mouse?

BERNARD WABER

Houghton Mifflin Company Boston

for my granddaughter
Rachel

For information about this and other Houghton Mifflin
trade and reference books and multimedia products,
visit The Bookstore at Houghton Mifflin on the World
Wide Web at http://www.hmco.com/trade/.

Library of Congress Cataloging-in-Publication Data

Waber, Bernard
  Do you see a mouse? / by Bernard Waber.
  p.   cm.
  Summary: Everyone at the ultra-fancy Park Snoot Hotel insists that
there is no mouse in the hotel, but the reader can see a mouse in
each illustration.
  ISBN 0-395-72292-6   PAP ISBN 0-395-82742-6
  [1. Mice — Fiction. 2. Hotels, motels, etc. — Fiction.]   I. Title.
PZ7.W113Do 1995   94-25172
[E]--dc20   CIP
    AC

Printed in the United States of America
WOZ 10 9 8 7 6 5 4 3

This is the Park Snoot Hotel.

One day, there was a big commotion in the hotel.

Shush! Don't let it get around,

but someone complained about seeing a mouse.

A MOUSE!!!!!

At the Park Snoot Hotel!!!!!

What a scandal! What a calamity!

Everyone at the Park Snoot said, "No.

No, no, no, there is no mouse here."

"No, no, no, there is no mouse here," said Simon, the doorman.

"Do you see a mouse? I do not see a mouse."

"No, no, no, there is no mouse here,"

said Mary Alice at the front desk.

"Do you see a mouse?

I do not see a mouse."

"No, no, no, there is no mouse here,"

said Marc, the concierge.

"Do you see a mouse?

I do not see a mouse."

"No, no, no, there is no mouse here," said Emil, the bellman.

"Do you see a mouse? I do not see a mouse."

"No, no, no, there is no mouse here," said Gaston, the chef.

"Do you see a mouse? I do not see a mouse."

"No, no, no, there is no mouse here," said Antoine, the waiter.

"Do you see a mouse? I do not see a mouse."

"No, no, no, there is no mouse here,"

said Bernadette, the telephone operator.

"Do you see a mouse?

I do not see a mouse."

"No, no, no, there is no mouse here,"

said Marika, the director of housekeeping.

"Do you see a mouse? I do not see a mouse."

"No, no, no, there is no mouse here," said Marcel in the hair salon.

"Do you see a mouse? I do not see a mouse."

"No, no, no, there is no mouse here,"

said Maurice, the hotel orchestra leader.

"Do you see a mouse?

I do not see a mouse."

"No, no, no, there is no mouse here," said Mercedes

in the flower shop.

"Do you see a mouse? I do not see a mouse."

"Rubbish!" said Sir Horace Morris, the world-famous explorer.

"I've seen baboons in the jungle, bats in caves,

but no, no, no, there is no mouse here. Take my word for it.

Do you see a mouse? I do not see a mouse."

"No, no, no, there is no mouse here—most definitely not!"
said Madame Eevah Deevah, the world-famous opera singer,
from her suite on the top floor.
"Do you see a mouse? I do not see a mouse."

"No, no, no, there is no mouse here,"

said Yolanda in the gift shop.

"Do you see a mouse? I do not see a mouse."

"No, no, no, there is no mouse here,"

said Mr. Josh Posh, the hotel owner.

"Do you see a mouse? I do not see a mouse."

"On the other hand," Mr. Posh went on, "to put everyone's mind at ease, I have engaged the services of Hyde and Snide, the foremost mouse catchers in the whole world, to look into this beastly matter."

HYDE & SNIDE
ELEGANT PEST
MANAGEMENT
1-800 CATCHEM   NEW YORK
PARIS
LONDON

"Never fear. Don't despair. Hyde and Snide are here,

mouse catchers extraordinaire—

crème de la crème, Rolls-Royce and all of that,"

the two announced themselves.

"Gentlemen, do what you must," said Mr. Posh.

Hyde and Snide began to look for the mouse.

They looked high. They looked low.

They looked inside.

They looked outside.

They thumped
and they bumped.

They tapped
and they rapped.

They looked here.

They looked there.

They looked everywhere.

No mouse.

"Do you see a mouse?"

said Hyde and Snide.

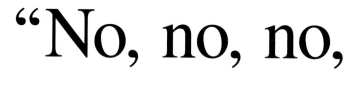

"No, no, no,

we do not see a mouse."

MOUSE!"

"Do you see a mouse?" said Hyde.

"I do not see a mouse," said Snide.

"I certify that there is no mouse here," said Hyde.

"I double certify," said Snide.

"Good-bye," said Hyde.

"Good-bye," said Snide.

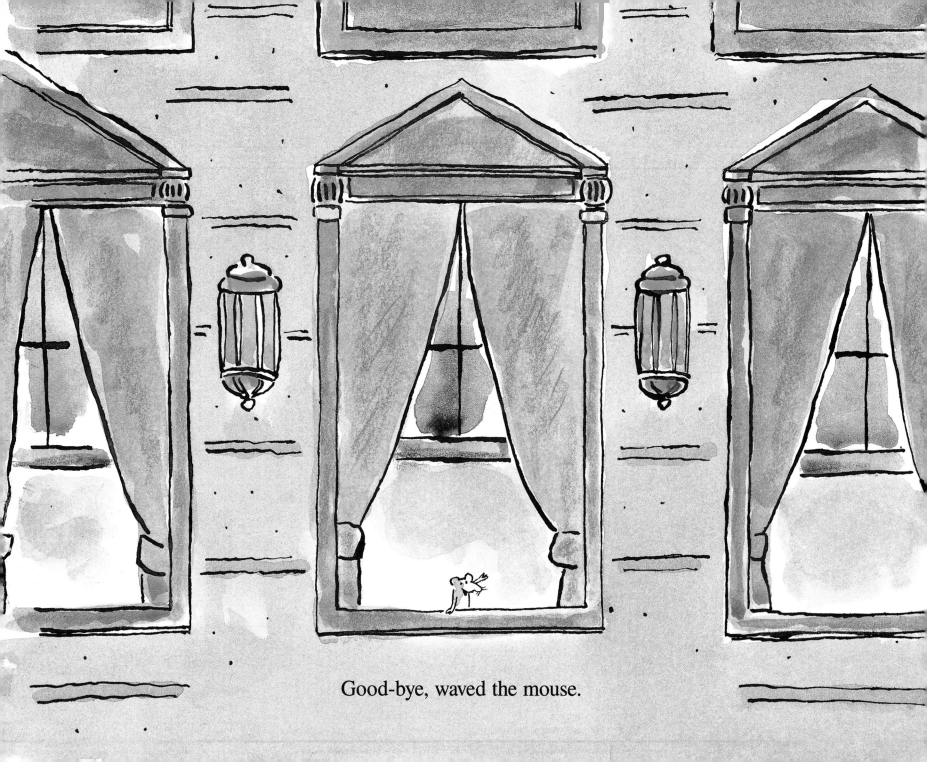

Good-bye, waved the mouse.